Letters
from Heaven

Also by Rachel Anderson

Tough as Old Boots
Princess Jazz and the Angels

Letters from Heaven

Rachel Anderson

mammoth

Thank you to the pupils at the Westlands
Secondary School, Sittingbourne, Kent,
for sharing with me their ideas about
dead grannies.

First published in Great Britan 1996 by Mammoth,
an imprint of Reed International Books Ltd,
Michelin House, 81 Fulham Road, London SW3 6RB
and Auckland, Melbourne, Singapore and Toronto

Copyright © 1996 Rachel Anderson

The right of Rachel Anderson to be identified as the author
of this work has been asserted by her in accordance with
the Copyright, Designs and Patents Act 1988

ISBN 0 7497 2776 4

A CIP catalogue record for this book is available
at the British Library

Typeset by Deltatype Ltd, Ellesmere Port, Cheshire
Printed in Great Britain by Cox & Wyman Ltd, Reading, Berkshire

Spring

Monday morning
about 8 o'clock

Hi Gran!

Just got that special letter from you. I was so surprised. No one ever writes to me normally. Then suddenly, here's two letters together! I couldn't believe my luck.

I recognised your handwriting straight away, and that blue paper you use. It's weird getting a letter from someone who's just died. But things have been weird all week.

As well as yours, there was the one from the lawyers, typed on posh paper in a big white envelope as though I'm someone really important. I didn't understand what it was about. Mum must have known. Did you tell her about it before? She was looking at me all worried over the top of the Weetabix packet when Dad brought the post in from the hall. They both sat there watching me opening the envelopes. They looked like they were half smiling and half about to cry.

Anyway, just wanted to say thanks. I'll write again properly after school.

Love from your own favourite person,

Katie XXX

Summerhill & Summerhill LTD,

SOLICITOR & COMMISSIONERS FOR OATHS,

Family Lawyers since 1893,

127 The Street,

Frogsford,

East Norfolk NR27 OLP

20 April 1996

Dear Miss Woodbridge,

Owing to the recent and sad demise of your stepfather's mother, Mrs R L Chambers, we are now in a position to release to you the enclosed letter which was formally entrusted into our safekeeping on the 2nd day of January 1987 at which time, Mrs Chambers requested that, immediately upon her decease, it be forwarded to you.

Please accept our sincere condolences upon your recent sad loss. If we can be of any further assistance at this time, do not hesitate to call upon us.

We beg to remain,

Yours faithfully,

John S. Summerhill

John S. Summerhill

to: Miss Katie Woodbridge,

6 Pond Row,

Lower Frogsford,

East Norfolk NR27 0LJ

Magnolia Cottage,
The Street,
Frogsford.

1st January, 1988

My very dear and special Katie,

This will reach you at some, as yet unknown, time in the future. Its purpose is to remind you how deeply you are loved.

You have been the bright centre of my affection since the charmed day you first entered my life when you ran across the room to me and said, 'I've been wanting a granny of my own for ages.' I understand how things were not always easy for you and your mother up till that time.

Since I may no longer be on this earth to tell you when you are of an age to understand, let me say now what joy and sunshine you've been bringing me. These past months since your mother's marriage to Robert have been a period of unexpected wonder and delight.

So thank you, dear child, a thousand times over.

Heaven alone knows how long any of us have in this funny old world. But, naturally, I hope we both have a few more years ahead for getting to know one another even better.

As I write by my fireside on such a bright crisp New Year's Day, I am greatly anticipating your visit this afternoon when Robert brings you over for tea. So, in a moment, I shall get out the box of toys he played with as a boy, and some of his old nursery books for us to share.

Ever, in this life and the next, your loving friend, and chosen 'grandmother',

Rose Lily Chambers

P.S. And when the lawyer sorts out the bequests, there will be a small gift coming to you of a more enduring nature than a letter: a tangible memento to remember me by. However, I'd like to think you'll remember me anyway.

Yrs again,

RLC

Still Monday

It's after tea

Hello Granny,

It's me again. Only now I'm in my room. It's quieter up here. I can think better and I'm writing to thank you properly.

That letter is so lovely lovely LOVELY. I've read it three times and in a minute I'm going to read it again. It makes me feel all safe and happy to know that you already quite liked me all that time ago, when I was only three.

Actually I'm amazed you thought I was a sunny person because my mum's often told me I was a right pest. Up until she met Robert, that is. 'You were very difficult to handle when I was on my own,' she said. 'You really stretched me to the absolute limit.' Whatever that meant! I didn't ask her, in case she got in a strop. But I thought you could only stretch rubber bands, not people.

At first, I couldn't understand the posh typed letter that came with yours. Mum knew it was difficult because she moved the Weetabix packet so she could see me and whispered, 'It's from the lawyer. D'you want me to explain it to you?'

'No thank you,' I said.

It's rare enough getting a letter at all so I didn't want her taking over, did I? I know she's my mum, but sometimes she's very irritating.

Anyway, it was easy enough to guess what 'demise' and 'decease' mean. Maybe the lawyer didn't dare write 'dead' in case it upset somebody?

If I'd been any other person in my class, I probably wouldn't have known about 'condolences' either. But this morning Mr Briggs at the Village Store sent Dad and Mum a really nice card with a picture of flowers and some hands praying by themselves without a body and instead of saying 'Happy Birthday' it says 'Condolences'. So now I know it's another way of saying 'sorry'.

The lawyer wrote that I can call on him any time. But you can't go visiting people you've never met, can you? I was going to throw his letter away. Then I thought I might as well keep it with yours, which I'm putting in a special secret place on top of the wardrobe. I'm going to keep it for ever and ever so I can read it whenever I want.

With tons and tons of love from your chosen grandaughter,

Katie

By the way, not sure where to post this. Suppose I'll have to ask Mum, though she's a bit distracted at the moment because of Dad's relations coming to stay for the funeral.

A Letter from Heaven

My dearest little friend Katie,

Always remember how much I loved you.
And don't miss me too much, will you?
 Don't be sad.

With my love,

Rose Lily Chambers

My room
Late at night

Dear Granny,

That was an amazing note you sent me, straight into my head.

Was it real?

How did you do it without anybody else noticing? Will you send me another? I do hope so.

But oh, Granny, what a funny idea. Course I don't miss you. Why should I? Not now I can write to you whenever I want.

Don't worry, I'm not sad either. Unlike your cousin Priscilla who's come to stay and keeps sniffing into her hanky all the time. Your brother Edwin is also staying here for a few days.

Night-night for now, love and kisses from me,

Lily-Rose XXX

Please note: in memory of you, I've decided to change my name. From now on I'm going to be Lily-Rose.

Lily-Rose

Saturday morning
Raining

Hello Granny,

I'm lying in bed listening to the rain on the window and wishing it was time to get up. Today's funeral day. So I'm really excited. It'll be my first. I wonder what it'll be like.

They didn't want to take me. Your cousin Priscilla (who says I've got to call her Aunt Priscilla even though she isn't) says, 'It won't be at all suitable. She'll make a fuss and upset everybody.'

I don't know why she thinks that when it's her who's been doing all the upsetting. 'She's like a leaking tap,' Mum says.

I shan't cry. What's the point? It'll all be much too interesting.

Yesterday we went into town to order the wreaths. Dad and Mum chose roses. Then Dad said I should choose a wreath too, which could be specially from me. I really like him, even though he's not my real dad. He always treats me like I'm human, not just some kind of nuisance.

The florist had a catalogue with all the different styles of wreath she can make. I've chosen the one that's shaped like a teddy bear. It'll be made of lots of small flowers all pressed close together to look like fur, and another kind of flower for eyes. In the picture it looks nice and if it was going to be my funeral that's definitely the one I'd want. There'll be a card round its neck. I've already written the message. I've put, 'For my dearest dearest Granny' and I've signed it, 'Love from Katie' because I didn't know how to explain to Dad and Mum about how I've changed my name to be more like yours.

Dad'll be going with his aunts and uncles in a hired car with a chauffeur. For some reason (Aunt Priscilla actually) I'm not allowed to go with them. Mum and I have to go in our ordinary car.

At least Mum's got me new socks and white ribbons. I wanted black like the grown-ups' clothes. But Aunt Priscilla says, 'Black is no colour for a child. Sombre but sensible is how she should be.'

So I've got to wear my boring school skirt and sweater. I wanted to wear the red velvet dress you got me last Christmas. (It was too long and you hemmed up the bottom. Remember?) It's my favourite because you chose it. But Aunt Priscilla said, 'Perhaps someone would explain to the child that it's not some disco party she's going to, but a service for the burial of the dead.'

Oops. There's Mum calling. Time to get up for breakfast.

Why didn't you answer my letter? Please get back to me if you can and tell me if you're all right, and what it's like, and what you have to eat. I asked Mum about it. She said dead people don't need to eat. But Dad said you probably feast eternally on the foods of heaven. I think he only meant it as a joke but

Aunt Priscilla cried and told him he was a cruel man.

Love from your

Lily-Rose

The Great Hereafter

Nevernever Land

Dear Lily-Rose

I am well thank you. Your father is entirely correct, the food is both plentiful and delicious. Already I have consumed ambrosia, milk and honey, clambake, sugar plums, scrag end, langoustine, locusts, Turkish delight, angel delight, tipari pomegranates, mangos, passion fruit, dewberries, Welsh rarebit, Jerusalem artichokes, ladies' fingers, fairy cakes and innumerable other delicacies.

As ever, your affectionate grandmother,

Rose Lily Chambers

My room
Sunday afternoon

Oh my own Granny,

You're the only person I can tell. It didn't turn out one bit like I expected. It was just so awful.

Mum and I got to the chapel a bit after the others because of parking. I thought we'd be sitting at the front so I'd be able to see properly. But Aunt Priscilla and your other relations had all the front pews. There were tons of other people there too. Who were they? You told me you didn't have that many friends left because of being so old. You told me that's why I'm special to you because I'm the one person who came to see you every single day since we first met.

Mum said, 'Well, that's families for you. Ignore an old lady when she's alive. All over her once she's gone.'

When we stood up for the singing, I saw the coffin. It was heaped with flowers. At first I thought it looked beautiful, like an indoor garden, but then I saw they were all wrong. They weren't like proper flowers. They were stiff and tidy, more like plastic. They didn't even smell. Someone put the teddy bear wreath right on top so you couldn't miss it. It looked awful. Why did I choose such a stupid flower bear? I know you won't like it.

I said to Mum in a whisper, 'Those aren't the sort of flowers Granny likes.'

Uncle Edwin turned round and told me to show a little respect for the departed.

I said, 'I am. And my granny hates flowers like that. She likes wild ones. Everybody knows.' Only I didn't whisper it. I shouted it out at the top of my voice so you'd hear me above the singing. But it only made everybody sing louder.

I tried to remember the names of your favourite flowers. I could only think of the easy ones like buttercups.

People were shushing at me and glaring at Mum.

'Completely undisciplined,' said Aunt Priscilla. 'What can you expect of a child from her background?'

I began to cry. Mum had to take me out.

I heard someone say, 'Poor little moppet. Missing her old nan I expect.'

But it wasn't that. It was because of the flowers being wrong. And anyway, I never call you 'Nan', do I?

The grown-ups don't understand anything. And I missed out on seeing you being buried because Mum said we'd got to hurry home.

She drove really fast. She had to get everything ready because after the funeral there was a horrible party with tons of food – fruit cake, hundreds of sandwiches, scones, shortcake, crisps, sausage-rolls. It was meant to be for you. I said that was stupid because you wouldn't be coming. And even if you were you don't like sausage-rolls.

All the people from the funeral came

pushing in like a herd of hungry elephants. It got so crowded they could hardly move.

When they'd gobbled up all the food, Dad got out the sherry. And they talked louder and louder, mostly about you.

It felt like being in a nightmare. None of them seemed to realise that I'm your special person. So I went outside and sat on the swing.

And suddenly I knew what you wanted, to make up for it being such an awful day. I ran round the garden and picked you the best bouquet in the world, so huge I could hardly get my arms round it. Daffodils, dandelions, bluebells, periwinkle. And some of the white fluffy stuff that's beside the compost heap. I do hope you'll like it. Only I'm not sure where to put it to stop the flowers wilting.

I liked being outside on my own. But Great Uncle Edwin saw me through the dining-room window and came shuffling out. He patted me on the head as though I were a pony. He said, 'Giddy up, girl. Chin up.' I think he was trying to say sorry for having told me off in the chapel.

I know he's your brother and all that. But I hope he'll be going soon so we can get back to normal like we used to be.

I'm glad I can write and tell you things. And I like it when you tell me things back inside my head.

Love and kisses from your own,

Lily-Rose (Katie)

Love and Kisses from your own

(Kitten)

Summer

The Garden of Eternal Rest

Somewhereovertherainbow

Dearest chosen child,

Do not fear about the flowers wilting. Here, all blooms last for ever, at the peak of their perfection. And of the many floral tributes, your gloriously flamboyant offering was by far and away the most delightful. It reminded me of the walks when we went across the Green and down Hollow Lane when I taught you the names of the wild flowers.

Remember how I told you to look closely and see how the bluebell is so named because of the little bells growing upon the stem? Here in the garden of rest, they chime the hour with an enchanting tinkle. Remember I showed you how forget-me-nots are like pale stars at twilight, each with its shining golden centre? Here, they twinkle like lamps in the evening.

The misty flower which grows in such profusion around your father's compost heap is the wild chervil, or cow parsley which scents the air of eternity like newborn baby's breath.

You will grow accustomed to Edwin's ways if you are patient. He may miss me a great deal at first. I took care of him from the day of his retirement. And now he is on his own.

Now you should sleep, my dear.

Sweet dreams.

Ever, your affectionate Granny,

Rose Lily

Summerhill & Summerhill LTD,

SOLICITOR & COMMISSIONERS FOR OATHS,

Family Lawyers since 1893,

127 The Street,

Frogsford,

East Norfolk NR27 0LP

20 May 1996

Dear Miss Woodbridge,

Further to our communication of 20 April, we are happy to inform you that, although probate has not yet been obtained on the estate of Mrs Rose L. Chambers of which you are a beneficiary, we are nonetheless in a position of being able to release to you, at this early stage, the Victorian-style silver-plated ink-stand which she bequeathed to you.

Assuring you at all times of our best intentions.

Yours faithfully,

John S. Summerhill

John S. Summerhill

to: Miss Katie Woodbridge,

6 Pond Row,

Lower Frogsford,

East Norfolk NR27 OLJ.

The kitchen table
The kitchen
Friday evening

Hello Granny!

Wow! The ink-stand and pen is the most terrifically best present in the world. Thank you tons and tons. I never thought you'd give me such an important present.

It's a sign, isn't it, that you want me to keep writing? Yes, I'm sure it is. So I'll use it every day.

Dad says it used to belong to his grandmother. Aunt Priscilla says it's a priceless heirloom and should've been kept within the family. She reckons that I don't count because I'm only a step. Luckily, Dad doesn't agree with her on everything. He's filled up the ink-wells for me with blue ink in one and red in the other. I can write to you with a different colour each day, depending on how I feel. As you see, today's a red ink day. Even though hc's not my real dad, quite often I like Robert better than Mum. The scratchy pen's a bit difficult to get used to. Dad says it needs a new nib, only they don't stock them in the Village Store.

Love you heaps,

Take care,

Lily-Rose

By the way, tomorrow at school we're going to learn Proper Letter-Writing. Aunt Priscilla said, 'In my day teachers taught sensible things.' What a grump. But she's leaving tomorrow (thank goodness). Uncle Edwin's still here, sleeping downstairs because he can't manage the stairs. Hope he'll be leaving soon too, so we can get back to normal.

6 Pond Row
Lower Frogsford
East Norfolk NR27 0LJ

24th July

Dear Granny,

I haven't heard from you for such ages. I suppose you're busy and it's really terrific in eternity with time to do all those things you always said you wanted to do and never had time for, like learning Hebrew, Arabic, Sanskrit. And I expect it's lovely weather, isn't it? And all your aches and pains are going away?

First day of school holidays tomorrow. So please send me a letter, or better still lots of letters.

Love from

Lily-Rose

6 Pond Row
Lower Frogsford
East Norfolk NR27 0LJ

26th July

Dear Granny,

Got to tell you about Mum. She's being such a pain, going on about how difficult things are. As though she was the only one with feelings. I can't bear the way she is at the moment. (I know it's all right to tell you because she's not your daughter. I'd never say anything nasty to you about Dad.)

This morning she snapped at me like I was a grubby bed-bug. Dad says she's a bit overtired because of Uncle Edwin. Well, it was her idea that he better live with us since he can't stay with you and they can't think what else to do with him.

I said, 'Actually, Granny's not gone. She's

still around. This morning, at breakfast, didn't you see her?'

You were here, weren't you? You popped round with some of your plum jam. I smiled at you and you smiled back. I knew it was you even though I couldn't quite see you so I wasn't frightened.

Mum got furious. She slammed the teapot down on the table. 'Of course she wasn't here. Why do you exaggerate all the time?'

After that, you sort of disappeared. Where do you go? I wish you'd taken Uncle Edwin. It feels like he's taking over our home. Not that he ever does anything, just sits, waiting for meals and staring. If supper's two minutes late he starts looking at the clock and grunting. Did you know he slurps his tea? And burps?

With love from

Lily-Rose

6 Pond Row
Lower Frogsford
East Norfolk NR27 0LJ

3rd August

Dear Granny,

URGENT MESSAGE ! ! ! ! !

You MUST tell them you're coming back otherwise you're going to end up with nowhere to live.

This morning Dad said, 'Mum and I are popping down to Magnolia Cottage to make a start on the clearing up.' He doesn't call it Granny's house any more.

Mum said, 'I expect you'd rather not come. You stay here and watch telly with your uncle. That'd be best.'

I said, 'What d'you mean, clearing up?'

Dad said, 'We've got to get it ready for the

new people.'

I said, 'You can't touch her things. She'll need them.'

Dad stroked my head, quite kindly but more as though I was a sick cat instead of a human person. 'No Katie, not any more she won't,' he said. I do like him a lot. But lately, he's been very distant as though he's always worrying about other things, and not noticing me at all.

'Dad!' I said. 'You don't understand. She's changed her mind. She's moving back.'

They're so thoughtless, those two. What shall I tell them?

Love from

Lily-Rose

6 Pond Row
Lower Frogsford
East Norfolk NR27 0LJ

29th August

Dear Granny,

Nearly the end of the holidays. Thank goodness. It's been so boring. I'm almost looking forward to getting back to school. We didn't go away anywhere because of You-Know-Who.

Just thought you'd also like to know, Mum and I went to visit your grave again today. Didn't want to. I said, 'What's the point?'

Mum said, 'Somebody has to make it tidy. And it's not going to get done by the fairies, is it?'

I said, 'You go then, if you want to so much. I'm not hanging around in a grave-yard.'

But of course I did go. I don't like her going off without me. There's more spooky corners at home than there used to be, even when the sun's shining.

So we both trogged down there. I sulked all the way so she had to be cheery for both of us.

'We'll tidy it up,' she said. 'And make it look nice, as though somebody cares.'

'Please yourself,' I said.

She's always complaining she's got too much tidying up to do. And now she's taking on another place to tidy. She really gets on my nerves.

Love from

Lily

Please note: Decided Lily-Rose is too long. So I'm shortening it to Lily. Hope this is OK?

Autumn

6 Pond Row
Lower Frogsford
East Norfolk NR27 0LJ

1st October

Dear Granny,

Mum made me go with her to the Garden Centre this morning to buy spring bulbs. They're for you, to plant on your grave.

I like all the wheelbarrows and plants and rose arbours and bird-feeders because it reminds me of your garden where there was always so much growing and nesting and burrowing going on. But I wasn't going to let her know.

The bulbs were heaped up in wooden tubs with photos over them to show what they'll look like when they've grown.

'Which ones, Katie?' Mum said. 'You choose.'

I remembered the horrible flower bear I chose.

I said, 'I'm no good at choosing.'

But I could see that the crocuses looked best. Purple, goldish yellow, white, pale blue. They reminded me of that time you planted all those crocuses under the tree, just for me. D'you remember? In the shape of a number six. So when they came up, I could read my age in flowers in the grass. I wasn't going to tell Mum about that either.

She said, 'So what colour d'you think Granny would like?'

'She's dead,' I said. 'So how should I know?'

After the Garden Centre, we went straight up to the cemetery. Mum said we'd put the bulbs in straight away to give them a good chance. I let her do it. I sat and watched all the time she was scratching with her little trowel all over the top of your grave, then digging up the earth and burying the little brown bulbs.

I said, 'Granny's not interested in ordinary

crocuses.'

'Isn't she?' Mum smiled.

'Where she's gone they have much better flowers. They have gillyflowers.'

'What?'

'In great radiance.'

'Gillyflowers?' Mum looked surprised. 'Where d'you learn about a thing like that?'

So do you have gillyflowers? Or was I making it up?

Please answer.

Love from

Lily

6 Pond Row
Lower Frogsford
East Norfolk NR27 0LJ

11th November

Dear Granny,

Mum and I aren't getting on too well. We've just had another stupid argument. Why do we fight all the time? I can't think straight. It's always worse when Dad's away.

It was about your letters. Since it involves you, I'll have to tell you.

After supper, she asked me to help clear the table and take Uncle Edwin his cup of tea, he always has to have his cup of tea, milky, two sugars. Then he just sits there in front of the telly. He has the volume up so loud.

'Why me?' I said. 'Always me. I'm not your slave.'

'No dear,' she said. 'Of course not. But I'd

still like a bit of help. We're all part of the same family.'

'What about him?' I said. 'I haven't noticed him lifting a finger to help. He's the one who makes the most mess. Why doesn't he ever help?'

'Because he's an old man.'

I said, 'Granny was old too. But she never sat around like a great bear all day.'

Mum sighed. 'You know he only breaks things.'

'Oh all right.'

We'd almost stopped arguing. It was going to be fine. I said, 'In a minute I'll help. As soon as I've finished my letter.' And I ran upstairs.

That set her off like a burglar alarm. She came after me. She stood at the bottom of the stairs shouting.

'Letters, letters. So where are these wonderful letters you go on about? I've never seen them.'

'They're to me, not you. That's why you haven't seen them.'

'It's just your excuse isn't it? To sit up in your room moping.'

'I don't mope. I write to Granny. And I know she writes back. At least she understands me.'

'Really! We've had all this out before. Of course she can't write back, you silly girl. They're just in your head.'

'They're not! They're not!'

I slammed my door. And I looked for your letters. I thought I kept them in a big pile tied with the white ribbons I wore at your funeral. I know I had them there.

I looked in the chest of drawers where I keep my old dolls. I looked under the bed. I looked in the wardrobe. I looked behind the books on my shelf. I pulled every single book down in case your letters were hidden between the pages.

But I couldn't find them anywhere.

Downstairs, Mum cleared the table herself.

'Well?' she said. She looked cross. 'So where are they?'

'I don't know,' I said. 'They've gone. Someone's stolen them.'

Oh Granny, I don't know what to do. How am I going to get them back?

Lily

6 Pond Row
Lower Frogsford
East Norfolk NR27 0LJ

13th November

Dear Granny,

Something so bad's been happening. It frightens me.

Your face has started to fade. I'm forgetting what you look like. I don't know how to get it back. I ran down and looked at the photo of you in the shiny frame on the sideboard. But it still didn't really help.

If I forget your face, next thing I'll begin to forget you. You've got to help me.

Love from

Lily

Winter

6 Pond Row
Lower Frogsford
East Norfolk NR27 0LJ

1st December

Dear Grandmother,

You've gone so quiet lately. You hardly ever write to me. You can't just drop me like this. Please come back, even if it's only once to say goodbye properly.

I remain, sincerely, your grandaughter,

Lily

Nirvana

Elysian Fields

Land of Beulah

My Dear,

You know that I cannot return. Do not allow yourself to wish for impossible dreams. They will not help you. I was glad that I survived long enough to witness my son's happiness when he met your mother. I am glad that I had a full life. But I was not sad when it was over.

Ever your affectionate Grandmother,

RLC

6 Pond Row
Lower Frogsford
East Norfolk NR27 0LJ

3rd December

Dear Mrs Chambers,

Of course you could come back if you chose to. You once told me that anybody can do anything if they put their minds to it. '"Can't" usually means "Won't".' That's what you said. So stop messing and get on with it. Because I'm running out of patience.

Have changed my name back to what it was. Hope you don't mind. Actually, I don't even care if you do mind. Lily was a silly old-fashioned name. So was Rose.

Yours sincerely,

Katie

TO MY EX-STEP-GRANDMOTHER,
IN PARADISE OR WHEREVER IT IS YOU
THINK YOU ARE.

I am getting really very annoyed by your lack of decent communication. So I shan't call you Dear, and I certainly shan't be calling you Granny. (And anyway, you never were my real grandmother.)

You dying was all very well at the beginning. Quite a novelty. But now I realise you did it deliberately, to check us out and see how much everybody cared. That was a really mean trick to play.

What makes you think you had the right to upset a whole family? Even your own brother? I mean, I don't find Uncle Edwin much fun, but he's human. It's terrible to see an old man cry.

So even if you were thinking of coming back, DON'T BOTHER!

Good riddance is more like it. I've got better things to do. And when I think how I used to walk down the lane, just to visit you, just to help you make scones, just to play with Dad's old toys, just to listen to you reading me stories, just to go out into your garden to look for snowdrops – it makes me sick. What a waste of time! I could've been doing loads of other MUCH MORE INTERESTING things.

Signed,

Ms Katie Woodbridge

9th December

Dear Granny, Dear Granny, Dear Granny,

I do miss you so much. I do. I do. I do.

I didn't know it'd get this bad. If only you were still alive. Then I'd come round and sit by your fire like I used to when things got bad and you'd make it all right again.

Now there's nothing. There's just empt-iness stretching ahead till the end of time.

From your own,

Katie

The House of Gloom
6 Gloom Row
Gloomy Street
Gloomford

10th December

Dear Granny,

OK then, so even if you won't get in touch with me any more, in fact even if you're not listening, I'm still going to tell you about things.

As I expect you know, it's nearly Christmas. Maybe not where you are. But it is round here. At school, we've decorated our classroom and been practising carols for our end of term presentation. The Infants are doing their nativity play on Wednesday. They're ever so sweet.

Dad's not had to be away so much lately. It ought to make things better. Trouble is he and

Mum don't seem very interested in anything, not even Christmas. They're tired and boring all the time.

I actually heard Mum tell Dad she couldn't face the preparations. Isn't that miserable of her? What made it worse was that he agreed.

'Yes, dear. We'll not bother with a big showy Christmas this year, will we? It wouldn't be right.'

The fact is we never had a showy Christmas. We always had an ordinary good family one. I bet you can remember because it was always the same, last year, and the year before that, and before that. Ever since I was three. You used to come over and take me to church. Mum and Dad stayed at home and got on with the dinner. And then by the time we came back Uncle Edwin would've turned up. And after our dinner, we used to come over to your house, didn't we? And you always gave me a new board game and we'd all play it together.

Only it can't be like that this year. It's going

to be awful, them not bothering, Uncle Edwin sitting there fidgeting if the meal's not on time. And me fed up. Mum hasn't even got a tree and she just leaves the Christmas cards in a pile without even putting them up. It's a disgrace.

How I do wish you were still here. I'm sure if you'd really loved me you wouldn't have let yourself die. If only you'd known how much we all need you.

Gloomily, from me, your very own,

Lily-Rose

Trapped for ever in this Terrible UnChrist-massy House of Gloom.

Somewhere Celestial

My Dearest Child,

There are many ways of loving. Sometimes loving is about choosing.

Your Mother and Father chose each other, but only for a lifetime.

Perhaps you could find it in your heart to choose someone, just as you once chose me, who needs a small share of love.

Perhaps you will not even have to seek very far.

I remain, ever your affectionate grandmother,

Rose Lily

6 Pond Row
Lower Frogsford
East Norfolk NR27 0LJ

12th December

Dear Granny,

Thanks for the message. I didn't really understand what you were on about. But then this very afternoon something quite amazing happened. Because of the carol rehearsal, I got home from school early. Mum wasn't in. Only daft old Uncle Edwin. Asleep as usual in his chair in front of the telly. I looked at him with his wispy white hair and for half a moment he looked almost like the Father Christmas in town. And I thought, well, maybe it's not all his fault that he's sad and grumpy. I crept into the kitchen. I made a pot of tea and took him some.

I woke him up very nicely and gently. 'Here's your tea, Uncle Edwin,' I said. 'Two sugars.'

'Why goodness gracious me!' he said with a start, then pretended he hadn't been asleep. 'Turn that blessed thing down, will you girl?' He waved his stick at the telly. 'I've got to have a parley with you.'

'A what?'

'A parley-voo. Chat.'

I knew it was going to be about something awful I've done. It always is.

'Now my girl. Listen here. Glad we're on our own. Got a job to do, you and me together.'

'Oh?' I said. 'Look, here's your tea.' I thought he might be having one of his barmy turns.

'Not tea. Tree, girl. Tree. Can't have Christmas without a tree can we? Got to be a surprise though. Got to get it when the old girl's out.' (He meant Mum.) 'Come on. Let's get moving. Got the dosh here.' He patted his wallet.

I couldn't believe it. Uncle Edwin wanting to go outside into the fresh air and find a tree. And not just find one but *buy* one.

I helped him into his greatcoat, and his scarf and his hat and his gloves and we set off.

It was horrible outside, sleeting and halfway to dark. But he wouldn't give up. Shuffling and slithering all the way into the wind. I had to hold on to his arm quite tight because I was sure he'd fall over and I'd get the blame.

We got down to the Village Store. They had the fir trees all stacked up outside. It looked as though they were growing there out of the path. Some of the sleet was settling on them. It was like a fairy forest.

'Now there's a beauty,' Uncle Edwin said. He chose the biggest and bushiest of all. 'Got good roots, this one. You can plant it out in the garden after.'

But it was much too big for either of us to carry. Mr Briggs, the greengrocer, said, 'This ain't no weather for you two young nippers to be out. Come on, I'll run you home in the truck.' He put the tree into the back, and me and Uncle Edwin squeezed into the cab with Mr Briggs. He's given us a bunch of mistletoe for nothing as well.

When we'd got the tree indoors, it made the whole house smell of green. It was delicious.

Mum got in and she was just flabbergasted.

'We've never had one that tall before! I hope we've got enough decorations.'

She went up to fetch them. They live in an old trainers' box on top of the wardrobe in my room. She was gone ages. I wanted to get going with decorating. So I went up to see what she was up to.

She was sitting on the floor reading all the letters I'd been writing to you.

'Oh no, Mum!' I said. I was shocked. I couldn't believe she'd do such a thing.

'Oh my little darling, my poor dearest girl,' she said. She flung her arms round my neck and she began to cry. 'I didn't know,' she said.

'I didn't realise you minded so very much. I thought it was just us who missed her so dreadfully.'

So I cried a bit too and we sat there on the floor and hugged and cried with all the sparkly bobbles round us. Then we heard a terrible wheezing noise like an old breathless bear coming slowly upstairs. It was Uncle Edwin.

He had two mugs of tea.

'Here y'are girls,' he said. The tea was stiff with sugar and he'd spilled most of it on the tray.

'But it's the thought that counts, isn't it ladies?' he said. He had to sit on the baby stool in my room for at least half an hour to recover from the effort.

With love from me,

The Happy House
Funtime Street
Jingle Town

18th December

Dear Granny,

I'll write this anyway because I still have to
say a few more things. But I shan't be sending
it anywhere. And I shan't be expecting a reply.

Things have got so much better. It seems
sudden. Perhaps it isn't really.

Every single afternoon, after his snooze,
Uncle Edwin goes out to the Village Store and
buys another special decoration. When I get in
from school, he's always sitting there in his
chair in the living-room with the fairy lights
on, pretending to be asleep. I have to look all
round the tree to find the new decoration he's
bought.

Today it's a tiny wooden rocking horse. I

had to search really hard. He'd hung it on a low branch right at the back. I had to crawl under the tree right through the presents.

It's a fantastic tree. Probably the best in the whole world. Christmas is so near now. I can hardly wait.

STOP. End. signed,

Lily

Boxing Day evening

26th December

Dear Diary. Whew. Christmas over. So much
to eat. So much chocolate. Such a full stocking.
I had some great presents. Uncle Edwin gave
me a big pink fluffy pig with a red spotted bow
round its neck and little shiny eyes. I'm a bit
old now for that sort of thing. He must think
I'm about four. But it was nice of him all the
same. And I'm going to try to learn to like it. At
least it's soft and cuddly. I hold it a lot, specially
when Uncle Edwin's looking to show him how
much I appreciate it.

As a matter of fact, it looks quite a lot like
him. So I've decided to call it Pig Edwin. That's
made Uncle Edwin ever so pleased.

The best present of all was from Mum and
Dad. It's a red leather book embossed in gold
letters on the front and with a brass lock with
a tiny key. It's a five-year journal.

Mum said, 'Better always keep it locked to make sure nobody goes reading your private things again.'

Unce Edwin said, 'That's a very sizeable notebook you've given the girl. How's she going to have enough things to fill all those pages?'

Dad said, 'Oh, I think our Katie can find enough things to write about.'

So I'm starting now.

Dad's just put some more coal on the fire. Uncle Edwin's having a snooze. Mum's up the other end of the settee reading the book she got in her stocking. (I got it for her. It's a love story.)

Outside, it's nearly dark but we're snug as bugs in here.

28th December

Dear Diary. Dad's made a desk for you, in my room, in front of the window. Granny's silver ink-stand is on it. I've re-filled the ink-wells with emerald green and purple to be ready for the New Year. There's a little place under one of the ink-wells where I hide the brass key.

I'm using the new pen from Aunt Priscilla (with green ink).

I began writing in here on Boxing Day. I wonder what'll be happening in my life five years less one day from this moment?

It's just started snowing. I can see the white blobs against the dark. Dad says it's below freezing and it'll probably stay.

31st December

Dear Diary. The snow's beautiful, specially when the sun's on it. So peaceful. The sky is pale blue like forget-me-nots.

Dad and Mum went up to the graveyard to put a wreath on Granny's grave. Holly and Christmas roses.

So I took Uncle Edwin out walkies. He needed two sticks because of the snow. I showed him what I've found at the bottom of the garden. Green tips of snowdrops poking through the snow.

'Look down there, Uncle Edwin. In a few weeks they'll be little white flowers there.'

'Ahaah,' he said. 'Flowers, very pretty.'

He seemed quite interested though I'm not sure if he saw what I was showing him.

'My sister was keen on flowers too. Poor old girl. Gone now, y'know.'

'Yes,' I said, and we came in and had our cup of tea and sat quietly. Just then I got

...ner of those messages from Granny. They feel like letters. They are in a way.

And this is what it seemed to say:

Dearest Grandaughter Lily-Rose,

Remember how much I have always loved you. Remember how precious you still are to those who love you. Remember how precious your love is to those you give it too. Goodbye my dear.

With deep affection, I am always, your grandmother,

Rose Lily